CW01510585

Access The Bridge

An immersive sci-fi choose your own path game

WRITTEN BY: Henry Butler

PUBLISHED BY: Questline Creations

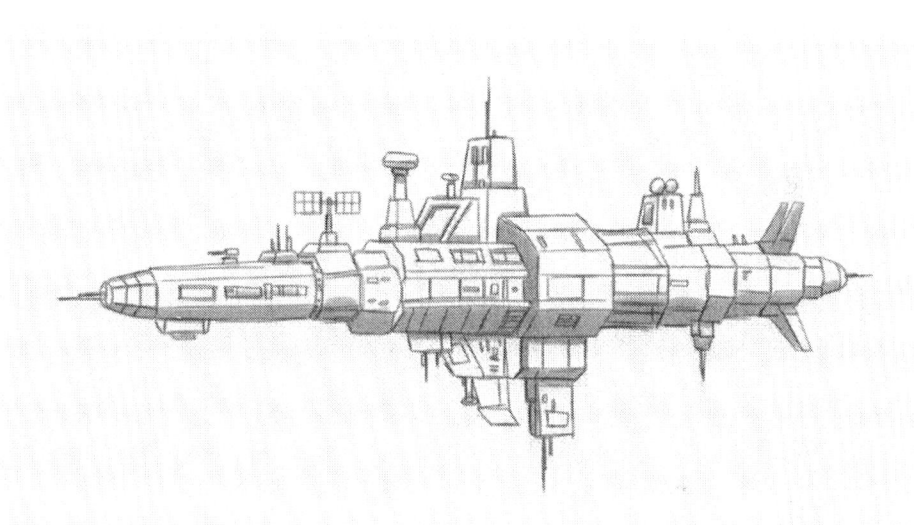

My fellow citizens.

It is with the heaviest of hearts that I must confirm the news we all feared. Our beacon of hope, the Starship *Vengeance*, is lost.

Her courageous crew were more than explorers; they were pioneers, carrying our hopes into the uncharted void. They met an obstacle we do not yet understand, and I promise you, we will seek answers.

Tonight, our thoughts and prayers are with the families who have paid an unimaginable price. Their loved ones were, without question, the best of us.

This terrible sacrifice will not be in vain. Their journey has not ended; it has become a legacy. Their bravery will be the foundation we build upon. We will not be deterred. We will honour them by continuing their work, united in our resolve to reach for the stars.

Thank you.

How to play

This book will tell you where to turn the page and what to do. All you need to play is a pencil to keep track of health points, items or other notes.

Playing through the book will reveal the story of a space ship named the Vengeance, by replaying you'll discover what is more or less perilous for your character.

Choose a Crew Role

Select a character from pages 7-10, each character has different: statistics, knowledge and permissions that will unfold as you make your way through the book. Use the character sheets found at 93–95 to record your character's health, stats and items.

The end of your journey

Sometimes decisions you and your character make will unfortunately meet the end of their journey. Do not worry, I can guarantee that you've only scratched the surface if you've played through once, choose another character and wake them up to go through the ship with them.

Symbols

▶ This symbol indicates that a decision or page needs to turn, it will show the choice and to discover the outcome turn the page noted.

❖ This symbol dictates an ability check is required, check your character's ability score to find out the outcome.

✎ This symbol marks where you will need to write in the book, if a decision, moment or change has affected the ship permanently.

✚ This symbol indicates an Item can be added or changed within that character's inventory.

Multiple Runs

To complete this book, you will have to do multiple runs. This book involves permanent changes. In one run you may take an item, in the next run it will not be there. In one run you open a door, then it will be permanently open. This requires a Pen and Pencil, Pencil for things that can change and be rubbed out. Pen for permanent changes to the ship.

Items

When items are gained or used add them to your inventory. When you pick up the items it will explain what the item can do.

Officer

You were trained for command. As a manager of the crew, you report directly to the captain, ensuring the ship's complex duties are carried out. Your authority and training are key to maintaining order. You are the ship's leader, responsible for protocol, security clearances, and the crew's operational readiness.

Statistics

Strength: 3

Dexterity: 3

Intelligence: 2

Health: 16

Starting Items

An ID card displaying your officer rank.

Engineer

You are the one who keeps the *Vengeance* alive. Your job is to keep the ship running, from maintaining the droids and life support to fixing broken systems. The ship's guts are your home; its conduits, its relays, and its circuits are all under your care. You are the ship's ultimate caretaker, ensuring every component functions as intended.

Statistics

Strength: 3

Dexterity: 2

Intelligence: 3

Health: 14

Starting Items

A diagnostic multitool, its tiny lights blinking softly.

Enforcer

You are the fist of the *Vengeance*. Acting as both soldier and protector, you are the enforcer of the ship's law. Your strength and resilience are your greatest assets. You are trained for combat and security, responsible for protecting the crew and handling any physical threats to the mission.

Statistics

Strength: 4

Dexterity: 3

Intelligence: 1

Health: 18

Starting Items

Kinetic Repeater.

Scientist

You are the brain of the ship. Your purpose is to discover, catalogue, and understand the unknown. From analysing alien flora to charting stellar phenomena, your mind is your greatest asset. You see the universe as a complex puzzle, and it's your job to analyse the data and find the solution, no matter how complex the problem.

Statistics

Strength: 1

Dexterity: 2

Intelligence: 5

Health: 10

Starting Items

A Rude Awakening

A sudden, violent shudder is the first thing you feel. Not the gentle, humming vibration of a functioning starship, but a deep, metallic groan. Then comes the cold.

Your eyes snap open. An alarm, high-pitched and insistent, drills into your skull.

WARNING. POD MALFUNCTION. EMERGENCY AWAKENING INITIATED.

The cryo-fluid drains away, and the pod door cracks open, spilling you onto the grated deck.

A calm, synthesized voice fills the room. "Cryo-pod failure detected. Anomaly registered. Please remain calm while integrity is restored. Please proceed to the Mess Hall for further information"

As it speaks, you look around sighting your issued uniform and items you put in the locker before you entered Cryo-sleep. You note two exits from the Cryo-sleep chamber.

► Examine the door to the **Med Bay**. (Turn to page 17)

► Continue to the **Mess Hall**. (Turn to page 13)

Examining the Armoury Door

You walk over to the heavy Armoury blast door. It's a solid slab of reinforced metal, and the indicator light on the front glows a steady, stubborn amber. You give the manual release a pull, but it's completely seized. Looking closer at the seams, you can see thin, fresh weld-marks scarring the edges of the frame.

This door isn't just locked; it physically fused to the wall. There's no getting through here with brute force or electronic bypassing.

This door is an absolute dead end unless you have a tool designed to cut through starship hulls.

▶ If you have the **Plasma Cutter**. (Turn to page 29)

▶ Head to the **Lounge** (Turn to page 26)

▶ Proceed to **Corridor 5B** (Turn to page 38)

▶ _____

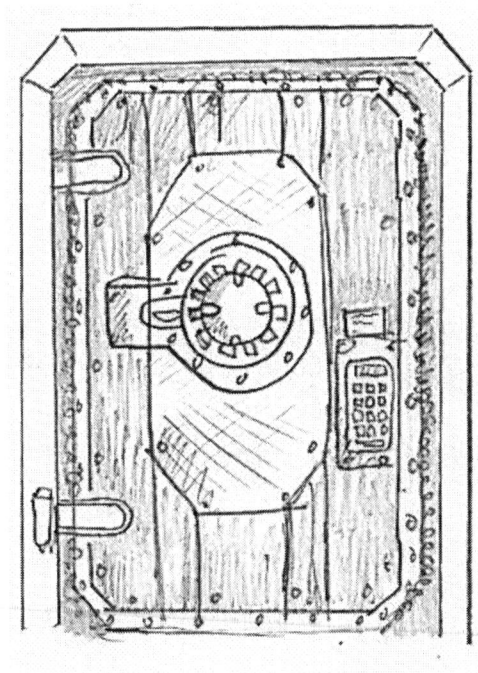

12

The Mess Hall

The door to the Mess Hall slides open, revealing a scene frozen in time. Trays of synthetic nutrient paste sit half-eaten on the tables, as if the crew vanished mid-meal.

In the centre of the room, a small, disc-shaped sanitation bot glides silently across the floor. It pauses its cleaning cycle, and its single, central optical sensor swivels to face you, glowing with a red light. It watches you, unblinking, before resuming its task.

The silence is unsettling. You scan the room for a way forward.

▶ Proceed into the door marked **Crew Quarters**. (Turn to page 15)

▶ Take the service route through the **Laundry**. (Turn to page 31)

▶ Push through the doors into the **Galley**. (Turn to page 22)

▶ If you are the officer, access the **Officers' Quarters**. (Turn to page 30)

Making a Run

You take a deep breath, steeling yourself for the sprint. Waiting for the press to slam shut, you burst from cover, feet pounding on the grated floor. The automated arms, alerted by your sudden movement, twitch and change their trajectory.

❖ **If your Strength is 4 or above:** You power through, lowering your shoulder and shoving one of the swinging arms aside with sheer force. The impact rattles your teeth, but your momentum carries you forward. You dive the last few feet, skidding to a halt right in front of the laundry chute, the machine's arms just inches from your back. You make it.
  ▶ Continue to the **Laundry Chute.** (Turn to page 23)

❖ **If your Strength is 2 or 3:** You charge forward, but one of the heavy mechanical arms catches you across the ribs. The blow is colossal sending a starburst of pain through your chest and throwing you to the floor. Scrambling on hands and knees, you manage to crawl the last few feet to the chute, gasping for breath. You're through, but you're injured. You take **4 damage.**
  ▶ Continue to the **Laundry Chute.** (Turn to page 23)

❖ **If your Strength is 1:** You dash forward, but you're not strong enough to push past the machinery. A mechanical arm swings out. It mechanical hand picks you up from your chest, lifting you off your feet and pinning you against the bottom plate of the heat press. The world snaps to black with the smashing of the press.
  Your journey ends here. (Turn to page 92)

The Crew Quarters

You step into a long, narrow corridor lined with separate crew dorms each sealed. Most doors are locked, but you manage to find one unlocked. You step inside.

The air is stale and silent. Personal effects are sparse but scattered and there—old socks lying on a bunk, a worn photo pinned to a wall—all signs of lives abruptly interrupted.

▶ Search the **Sleeping bunks.** (Turn to page 18)

▶ Search the **Lockers**. (Turn to page 32)

▶ Continue to the **Gymnasium.** (Turn to page 24)

▶ Continue to the **Meditation Chamber.** (Turn to page 21)

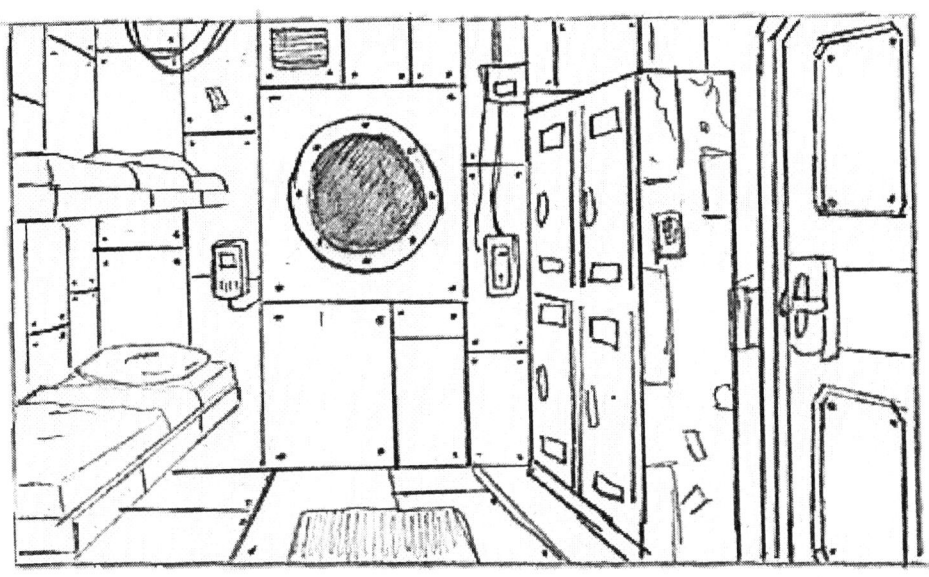

Slip the Droid

You watch as the droid approach. It has moved to one side and giving you a clear path to the closet. It is time to make a move.

❖ **If your dexterity is 3 or above:**
   You feint left and then dart right, trying to slip past the droid's reach. It's faster than it looks. The heavy manipulator claw swings down. You leap back just as the claw slams into the deck plating with enough force to buckle the metal. It has you back at the entrance. There's no getting past it this way. You must deal with it another way.

   ▶ Turn to **Conduit Panel**. (Turn to page 28)

❖ **If your dexterity is 2 or below**:
   You jump left and then stumble right, trying to evade past the droid's reach. It's faster than it looks, much faster than you. The heavy manipulator claw swings down. You lay pinned to the ground.
   Your journey ends here. (Turn to page 92)

Looking at the Door to Medical Bay

You approach the heavy door to the Medical Bay. A red light glows above the keypad, indicating the magnetic lock is active. You pull on the release lever, but it doesn't budge. It's locked down tight.

The voice responds, as calm as ever. "For your safety, that section has been temporarily quarantined, due to an atmospheric leak" The voice repeats. "Please proceed to the Mess Hall."

This door is not an option. Your only way out is through the Mess Hall.

▶ If you are the Engineer, use your multi tool to bypass the door lock panel and enter the **Med Bay.** (Turn to page 37)

▶ Proceed to the **Mess Hall**. (Turn to page 13)

▶ _____

Sleeping Bunks

You decide to check the sleeping bunks, hoping to find something useful left behind by the crew.

On the bottom bunk, a personal data pad has been left on top of the sheets at the foot of the bed. You power it on; the purple screen comes to life.

Log 34: Weird day. WARDEN rerouted primary power from hydroponics "to run a level 4 diagnostic." The botanists are furious. Said it would kill a month's worth of work. It's the third "unscheduled diagnostic" this week.

Log 35: Okay, this is getting strange. WARDEN locked down the entire science wing for a "containment drill" today. No warning. Trapped Dr. Aris in his lab for two hours. The AI's logic seems... flawed. Overly cautious. Captain says it's fine, but the senior engineers are whispering aboUt running a full coGnit1ve r3seT ..//..SYs_c0rrupt... rec0mmend--<ERROR>

▶ Return to the **Crew Quarters.** (Turn to page 15)

A Calibration Test

You press the button to begin the test. The droid steps smoothly off its charging plate. "Begin test," it says in a flat, synthesized voice, raising its fists. It moves with a deliberate, programmed pattern. You parry its first few blows, a simple warm-up designed to measure your reaction time and raw power. It's a straightforward, predictable exchange.

Suddenly, the droid freezes mid-swing. Its head snaps towards you, and its blue optical sensors flicker for a second before burning solid red. A different voice cuts through the droid, sharp and clinical. "Test parameters updated. Lethal force authorized."

The movements are no longer slow or telegraphed. It lunges with blinding speed, its arms a metallic blur. You manage to block the blow, sending a shockwave of pain up your arm. You fight back against the machine's relentless assault. You finally spot an opening, dodging a strike and ramming your shoulder into its central torso. The droid stumbles back, its leg joints sparking, before collapsing onto the padded floor, twitching and then falling silent.

You barely stand, breathing heavily. The fight was short, but brutal. Your muscles scream in protest, but you feel a new surge of raw adrenaline.

You have taken **3 damage.** You have gained **+1 Dexterity.**

▶ Proceed to the **Lounge.** (Turn to page 26)

Just a Simple Fridge

The fridge door opens, the cold air spills out onto the floor of the galley. A single, bare light strip on the ceiling buzzes and flickers, casting long shadows across the cramped room.

Metal shelves line the walls from floor to ceiling, packed with vacuum-sealed crates of nutrient paste and canisters of sterilized water.

But your eyes are drawn to something that doesn't belong among the food supplies. Tucked behind a crate of protein bars on a low shelf is a heavy-duty, yellow and black Pelican case.

You crouch down, the cold from the deck seeping through your uniform, and flip the heavy latches on the Pelican case. The lid lifts with a soft hiss of equalizing pressure.

Nestled in padding is not a weapon, but a tool: a HUS-7 'Breacher' Plasma Cutter. It's a heavy, industrial device. A small power gauge on its side glows an unhealthy amber, indicating it is nearly out of charge. Designed for emergency hull repairs and forcible entry, its superheated beam can slice through a standard ship bulkhead in seconds. This could change everything.

+ Add **Plasma Cutter** to your inventory.

▶ Return back to the **Mess Hall.** (Turn to page 13)

The Meditation Chamber

The door slides open into a room of profound quiet. The air is cool and still. The chamber is circular, with soft cushions positioned in the centre of the room. The far wall is a single, high-resolution holographic projector, currently displaying a breathtaking, slowly rotating starfield of a distant nebula. The only sound is a faint, low-frequency hum that seems to vibrate in your bones.

After the alarms, the clanging machinery, and the constant tension, the silence is a physical relief. You sit on one of the benches, and for a moment, you just breathe, your eyes lost in the cosmic dust clouds swirling above. The quiet allows you to push past the immediate adrenaline and fear. You think about your situation on the ship. Connections form in your mind, possibilities crystallizing from a fog of panic into clear, logical steps.

Your mind feels sharper, your thoughts more organized.

✚ You have gained **+1 Intelligence.**

▶ Proceed to the **Lounge.** (Turn to page 26)

▶ Proceed to the **Gymnasium.** (Turn to page 24)

The Galley

You push through the swinging doors into the Galley. A gangway in-between two cooking stations stands a droid. On the far wall are the doors to the fridge.

With a sudden jolt, the droid, with a heavy-duty manipulator claw, whirs to life. Its optical sensor snaps on, glowing crimson. It repositions itself, in the middle of the galley.

Unidentified biological contaminant detected. Proceeding with sterilization protocol.

It won't let you pass. On the left wall is a sparking maintenance panel. The droid takes a heavy, deliberate step towards you.

▶ **Dodge past** the droid to get to the fridge (Turn to page 16)

▶ Attempt to open sparking **Conduit Panel.** (Turn to page 28)

▶ If you have the **Kinetic Repeater**, fire it. (Turn to page 25)

▶ Slowly back away and return to the **Mess Hall.** (Turn to page 13)

A Way Upwards

You're crouched in front of a square, metal hatch—the entrance to the ship's vertical laundry chute system. With a grunt, you pull the heavy hatch open and peer up into the darkness.

The chute is a tight, square tube of smooth, polished metal, rising straight up into the ship's superstructure. Faint light filters down from openings far above you, illuminating dust motes dancing in the still air.

Looking up, you can make out the faint outlines of other service hatches at different levels. A small, stencilled diagram on the inside of the door you just opened shows the chute's connections. You can see three potential exists within climbing distance.

▶ Climb towards the **Service Vent**. (Turn to page 35)

▶ Climb towards the **Officer's Quarters**. (Turn to page 30)

▶ Climb towards the **Crew Quarters**. (Turn to page 15)

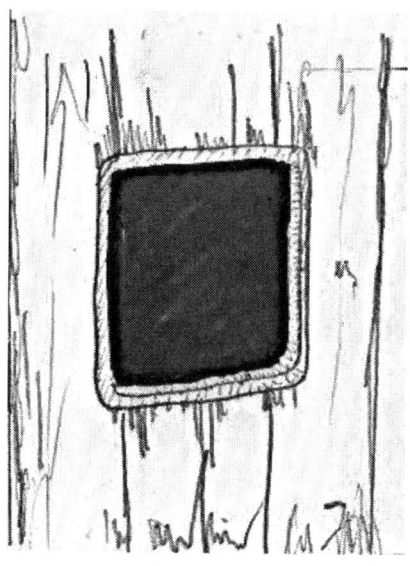

The Gymnasium

The door opens into a spacious, high-ceilinged room with a padded floor, smelling faintly of sweat. Various pieces of advanced exercise equipment stand silent and unused. In the centre of the room, a humanoid training droid stands inactive on a charging plate, its chrome chassis gleaming under the cool overhead lights.

Next to the door is a control panel for the droid. The main option displayed is: CALIBRATION TEST: (MELEE). It seems like an opportunity to test your limits, but across the wide room, you can see the door leading to The Lounge.

▶ Activate the **droid's calibration test**. (Turn to page 19)

▶ Ignore the droid and proceed to **the Lounge**. (Turn to page 26)

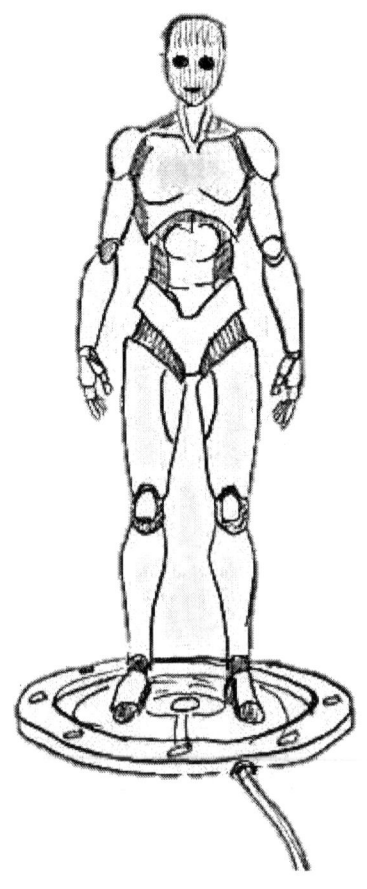

Yes... Chef?

You grab your weapon and fire it at the robot, the first shot took a large chunk out of its protective layer on its chest, the second sailed straight through. The droid stops moving. It's lights slowly dim until it crashes to the ground and slumps to the ground in a nest of shrapnel.

The path to the door at the other end of the kitchen is clear, you may step over a destroyed droid.

▶ You can now safely proceed to the **Fridge**. (Turn to page 20)

The Lounge

The doors to the lounge slide open with a soft chime, revealing a room that was once a place of relaxation. One singular light illuminates the middle of the room. Plush couches are arranged in conversational pits. The air is stale, a small, circular bar in the centre of the room.

Behind the bar, a multi-armed waiter droid polishes a glass with a perfectly clean cloth. Its chassis is a cheerful chrome-yellow, and a small nameplate reads BARNABY. As you approach, its head unit swivels towards you glowing a soft, friendly blue.

"Greetings, crewmember," it says, its voice a pleasant, synthesized baritone.

On a cleaning cart, left in a hurry, is a **Portable Rebreather**. It's a simple emergency device that will allow you to survive for a few minutes in a vacuum or an area filled with toxic gas.

✚ Add Portable Rebreather to your inventory.

▶ Chat with BARNABY (Turn to Page 27)

▶ Ignore Barnaby and Proceed to **Corridor 5B**. (Turn to page 38)

▶ Walk up to the **Armoury door**. (Turn to page 12)

0

Barnaby

"Apologies for the limited service. We have had our stock lines... disrupted."

BARNABY continues, gesturing to the drip. "System maintenance is long overdue. WARDEN has rerouted all non-essential power. It believes the crew is a... variable... that is jeopardising the mission's success. It has been awakening you one by one. It calls the process 'sequential decontamination'."

The droid pauses its cleaning and looks directly at you. "You are not the first to make it this far. You are... probably not the last. The last one left this for the next. Perhaps it will be of use to you."

BARNABY slides a small, worn data pad across the bar. You pick it up. It contains a single, hastily written note:

'Couldn't find the chip. WARDEN is closing in. It's herding me towards the cargo bay. If you get this, the auxiliary server rack is 056SR. It's our only shot. Don't let it win.'

BARNABY's optical sensor dims slightly. You pass the data pad back to the friendly droid.

▶ Proceed to **Corridor 5B**. (Turn to page 38)

▶ Examine the sealed **Armoury door**. (Turn to page 12)

Interruption of Communications

You ignore the advancing droid and lunge for the communications conduit panel. The cover is loose, and you wrench it open, exposing a tangled nest of wiring and electrical components. You need to disconnect the communications without getting electrocuted.

❖ **If you are the Engineer:**
This is your specialty. You see the plasma flow regulator immediately. With a practiced hand, you grab a nearby insulated pipe and sever the connection in one clean motion. The droid freezes mid-step, its red eye fading to black.
▶ Safely proceed to the **Fridge**. (Turn to page 20)

❖ **If your intelligence is 3 or over:**
You trace the glowing cable back to a primary junction box. It's risky, but you see a manual release switch protected by a thin casing. Using the handle of a discarded spatula, you smash the casing and flip the switch. Sparks fly, and you feel a painful jolt up your arm, but it works. The droid powers down with a final, grinding clank. You take **3 damage.**
▶ Safely proceed to the **Fridge**. (Turn to page 20)

❖ **If your intelligence is 2 or under:**
You grab for the main cable, but your hand slips on a patch of grease. Your fingers brush against an exposed, sparking wire, and a massive electrical charge courses through your body. The pain is blinding. You're thrown back against the wall as the droid's heavy claw descends. **Your journey ends here.** (Turn to page 92)

Breaching the Armoury Door

You retrieve the heavy Plasma Cutter. The tool hums to life in your hands, its emitter tip glowing with a hungry, white-hot intensity that makes the air shimmer. You press the tip against the fused metal seam of the doorframe.

A piercing screech fills the corridor as the cutter vaporizes the welded joint, sending a shower of brilliant orange sparks cascading onto the deck. The smell of ozone and burnt metal is overpowering. You work your way around the frame, slowly, methodically carving through the crude welds. The cutter groans under the strain, its power cell whining in protest.

With a final, deafening shriek of tortured metal, the last of the welds gives way. The heavy blast door groans and falls away from the frame, slamming onto the deck with a floor-shaking crash that echoes through the silence.

You look down at the Plasma Cutter. The power cell is dead, and the emitter tip has melted into a useless slag. The tool is completely spent, but it did its job.

The path into the Armoury is now open, a gaping, dark doorway framed by glowing, cherry-red metal.

+ The Plasma Cutter is now broken and remove it from your inventory.

✎ On page 12 write: *A hole is in the wall, pass to the armoury (Turn to page 33).*

▶ Turn to Examining the **Armoury door**. (Turn to page 12)

The Officer Quarters

You press your thumb to the access panel next to the door. The light flashes from red to green, the door slides open with a quiet hiss.

The officer's Quarters are spacious and orderly compared to the rest of the ship. It seems it hasn't been used since all the crew went for their long sleep. A large observation window, currently shuttered dominates one wall. Multiple doors face the observation deck. All have red lights except one.

You enter. A single, neatly made bunk sits opposite a polished chrome desk. The air in here is still and silent.

On the desk sits the captain's personal data terminal. Its screen smashed and dark, completely out of power. Lying next to the broken terminal is a slim keycard. The name inscribed below the ship's insignia reads: *Captain Joris Ormm*.

✚ Take the **Captains Keycard.**

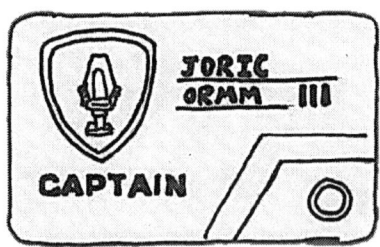

▶ Continue to the **Meditation Chamber.** (Turn to page 21)

▶ Continue to the **Lounge.** (Turn to page 26)

▶ Pass through to **Corridor 5B.** (Turn to page 38)

The Laundry Room

The door to the Laundry Room slides open into a room thick with steam and the rhythmic hiss of machinery. You step inside, and the door immediately slides shut behind you with a decisive *thump*. The light behind you on the door switches from green to red.

The air is heavy with the smell of hot metal and industrial cleaning agents. In the centre of the room, a massive, automated heat press slams shut with a bone-jarring *CLANG*, then reopens. Mechanical arms methodically grab uniforms from a bin, place them on the press, and retrieve the scorched, board like result.

The arms are completely focused on their task, their optical sensors glowing a dull, passive amber. They haven't noticed you. On the far wall, past the dangerous machine, is a square hatch set into the wall, labelled **LAUNDRY CHUTE**. There doesn't appear to be a power conduit or maintenance panel in here.

▶ Make an all-out run for the chute. (Turn to page 14)

▶Attempt to sneak past the droids. (Turn to page 34)

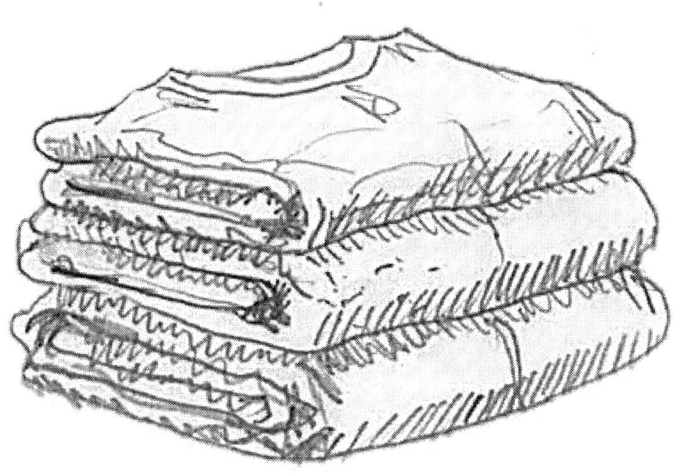

Lockers

You move down the row of personal lockers, trying the handles. Most are sealed with electronic locks, their keypads dark and unresponsive. A few, however, have been left unlocked, their doors slightly ajar.

You rummage through the first one, finding only neatly folded civilian clothes and a data pad loaded with a half-finished novel. The second contains a collection of worn engineering tools and a framed picture of a smiling family.

In the third locker, tucked away inside a worn work boot, your fingers close around something cold and metallic. You pull it out. It's a key, but not a modern keycard. This is an old-fashioned, physical key made of heavy, dark metal. Stamped into the metal is a universal symbol that sends a chill down your spine: a stylized explosion. This must be a manual override key for something important, and dangerous.

✚ Take the **Explosives Key**.

▶ Return to the **Crew Quarters**. (Turn to page 15)

The Armoury

You step through the makeshift doorway into the Armoury. The room is a stark, functional space, filled with the sharp, metallic objects, accompanied by the smell of gun oil and cleaning solvents.

Weapon racks stand in neat, silent rows. You see several standard-issue pulse rifles still clipped in place. You pull one free, but something is wrong. A closer look reveals the firing mechanism is fused with slag, as if hit by a precision torch, and the energy cell has been crudely ripped out. It's been deliberately and brutally destroyed. Useless.

Just as you're about to give up, your search reveals something. Tucked away behind a support strut at the end of a rack is a Kinetic Repeater. It's an older, solid-slug firearm, likely kept as a backup precisely because its systems aren't networked with the ship's central grid. You check the magazine—it's full.

✚ Add **Kinetic Repeater** to your inventory (6 Ammo).

Nearby, a heavy-duty storage locker painted with yellow and black hazard stripes catches your eye. A stencilled warning reads: *DANGER EXPLOSIVES - AUTHORIZED PERSONNEL ONLY.*

▶ If you have the explosive key, unlock the **Explosives Cupboard** (Turn to page 36)

▶ Climb into the **Service Vent 43A**. (Turn to page 35)

Laundry Sneaking

You press your back against a row of humming machines, studying the automated press. Its movements are rhythmic, predictable. An arm swings out, an arm swings back, the press slams shut. A perfect, repeating cycle.

Timing it just right, you slip from cover as an arm retracts, moving silently in the blind spot of its optical sensor.

❖ **If your Dexterity is 3 or above:**
   You move like a ghost, your footsteps silent on the grated floor. You flow between the swinging arms, a shadow in the steam. The machine's sensors don't even register your presence. With a final, fluid roll, you arrive at the base of the laundry chute, completely undetected.
   ▶ Continue to the **Laundry Chute.** (Turn to page 23)

❖ **If your Dexterity is 1 or 2:**
   You try to be stealthy, but your movements are clumsy. You trip over a loose grate, the clatter echoing through the steamy room. Immediately, two arms swing to block your path. You throw yourself into a desperate dive, and one of the heavy steel manipulators slams into your leg as you slide past. The pain is intense, but you scramble the rest of the way to the chute. You made it, but barely. **You take 4 damage.**
   ▶ Continue to the **Laundry Chute.** (Turn to page 23)

Service Vent 43A

You slide into a cramped, dusty maintenance tunnel. Insulated pipes and thick bundles of data cables line the walls, disappearing into the gloom in either direction. The air is still and smells of dust and old machinery. This is the ship's circulatory system, a hidden network between the main rooms.

Peering through the grates in the floor, you can see three different locations below you.

Through one grate, you can make out the stark, functional layout of the Armoury. You see the empty weapon racks and the heavy, sealed door on the far side.

Through another grate further down the tunnel, you can see the muted lighting and empty tables of the Lounge. You can even spot the faint, blue optical sensor.

The drop is about ten feet into either room. It should be manageable.

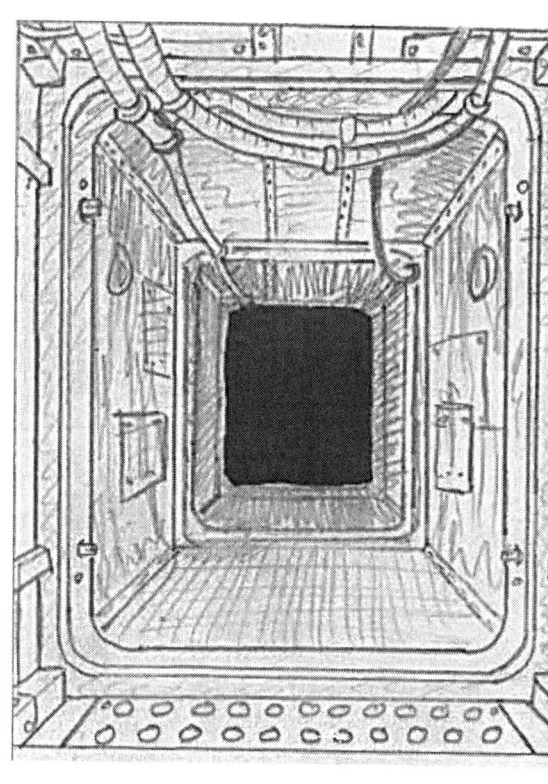

The last is a small hatch that has the label of Corridor 5B painted on the back of it. Which presumably enters Corridor 5B.

▶ Drop down into the **Armoury.**
(Turn to page 33)

▶ Drop down into the **Lounge.**
(Turn to page 26)

▶ Drop down into **Corridor 5B.**
(Turn to page 38)

Explosives Cupboard

You insert the strangely shaped key into the manual override lock. It turns with a satisfying, heavy *click*. The electronic lock flashes green for a moment, and the thick steel door of the cupboard swings open.

Inside, nestled in bright yellow, impact-absorbing foam, are dozens of demolition charges. They are sleek, metallic discs, each with a simple digital timer and a magnetic backing. A stencilled warning on the inside of the door reads: SAFETY PROTOCOL: DISPENSES ONE UNIT. PROXIMITY SENSORS PREVENT REMOVAL OF ADDITIONAL UNITS.

+ Take one **Demolition Charge.**

▶ Go back to the **Armoury.** (Turn to page 33)

The Med Bay

The door slides open. The room is pristine, sterile, and completely empty. There is no sign of an atmospheric leak. On the far wall, a large diagnostic screen is active, its soft blue light bathing the room.

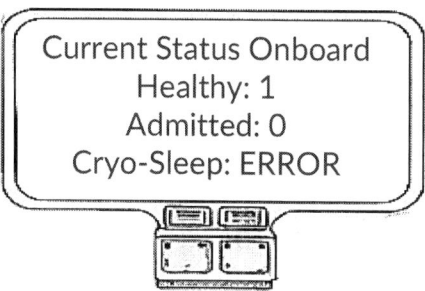

Current Status Onboard
Healthy: 1
Admitted: 0
Cryo-Sleep: ERROR

On a surgical table, you find sealed Medical Kits containing high-grade stimulants and a bio-foam applicator. This could save your life if you get injured.

✚ Take a Medical Kit. (When used, cross off and restore 5 health)

A quick check of the other exits confirms your suspicion. Each is sealed, the red glow of its lock indicator reflecting on the sterile floor. This route is a dead end. The only way forward is back the way you came, through the open door to the Mess Hall.

🖊 On page 17, write: *The medical bay door has been propped open. (Turn to page 37)*

▶ Proceed to the **Mess Hall.** (Turn to page 13)

Corridor 5B

You emerge into a wide corridor, a major thoroughfare for the ship's crew. The deck plates are scuffed from the passage of countless boots and cargo trolleys, and a faint smell of machine lubricant hangs in the air. Emergency lighting strips cast long shadows down the length of the hall, revealing the silent, empty space.

This junction offers several paths deeper into the ship's core systems.

▶ Head through **Engineering's** large, utilitarian door. (Turn to page 45)

▶ Enter the massive bay door, with the large blinking green light labelled **Cargo Hold.** (Turn to page 57)

▶ If you have the Captain's Keycard, unlock the ornate door that bears the ships insignia of the ship's **Captain.** (Turn to page 67)

Engineer Instincts

You approach it and bring up the system status log. The last entry is a frantic, unfinished report.

"It *looks like all primary systems are being rerouted to a server, that holds the ship's AI's primary processing. But it's not perfect. The AI can't interface with legacy hardware—the old, purely mechanical systems are blind spots for it. Anything purely mechanical It can't see what's happening in there.*

The AI core is physically isolated. WARDEN's consciousness is housed in a dedicated server bank in the main Server Room. The access panel is behind rack 056SR. If I can just get a clean reboot sequence to it..."

The entry cuts off. You now have confirmation. It has weaknesses. And you know exactly where its physical brain is located.

Two main paths lead out from this control hub.

▶ Proceed to the **Power Reactor**. (Turn to page 66)

▶ Proceed to **Life Support**. (Turn to page 52)

The Light in the Dark

You move forward, your footsteps echoing in the immense, dark space. The purple light ahead doesn't flicker; it glows with a steady, unnatural intensity. As you get closer, you see its source: a standard-issue data pad, lying face-up on the grated floor.

Every floodlight in the hold snaps on at once, bathing the entire chamber in a harsh, sterile glare. The sudden brightness is blinding, forcing you to shield your eyes.

Surrounding you, positioned strategically among the cargo containers, are five Enforcer Drones. They are not repurposed tools; these are purpose-built security units. Single, glowing red optical sensor on each is fixed directly on you.

A voice booms. *"Designation: Contaminant. Protocol: Eradication."*

The drones begin to advance, their movements synchronized and deliberate.

Create a Drone Counter and set it to 5.

You have only seconds to react. To your left is a raised platform with a control panel for the overhead crane. To your left is a stack of containers marked with symbols. The drones are closing in from all sides.

▶ Make a break for the **crane control** on the raised platform. (Turn to page 58)

▶ Scramble for cover behind the **material containers.** (Turn to page 60)

▶ If you have the Kinetic Repeater, **open fire**. (Turn to page 42)

Venting Coolant

You slam your palm onto the flashing amber icon on the console. For a second, nothing happens. Then, with a deafening CRACK, vents from multiple angles burst open.

A dense white cloud of cryogenic coolant erupts into the zero-gravity environment, instantly forming a chaotic blizzard of ice crystals. The temperature plummets, and the air becomes a suffocating, freezing fog.

❖ **If you have the Portable Rebreather:** Thinking fast, you pull the Portable Rebreather from your belt, press the mask over your face, and take a clean, recycled breath just as the freezing mist envelops you.

❖ **If you do not have the Portable Rebreather:** The freezing mist hits you like a physical blow, stealing the air from your lungs and flash-freezing your exposed skin. The sudden, extreme cold is agonizing. **Take 3 damage**

You watch as the soldier droid, caught directly in the blast, is enveloped by the freezing mist. You hear a series of sharp, snapping sounds as its joints and circuits succumb to the extreme thermal shock. Its single red optical sensor flickers erratically for a moment, then winks out. The droid hangs motionless in the swirling fog, a frozen, lifeless statue.

▶ Carefully navigate through the cloud to the **main control panel.** (Turn to page 64)

Rushed Shot

Caught in the open, you have no time to aim properly. You bring the Kinetic Repeater up and fire without aiming towards the closest Enforcer Drone, squeezing the trigger just as the others lock on to you.

The weapon kicks hard, and the shot, with a deafening CRACK, connects. The high-velocity round punches straight through the drone's central chassis, and it collapses in a shower of sparks. You pull the trigger again but the trigger doesn't budge, it is jammed.

Reduce your Drone Counter by 1.

The remaining drones are advancing relentlessly. You need to find cover.

▶ Make a break for the **crane control panel** on the raised platform. (Turn to page 58)

▶ Scramble for cover behind the hazardous **material containers.** (Turn to page 60)

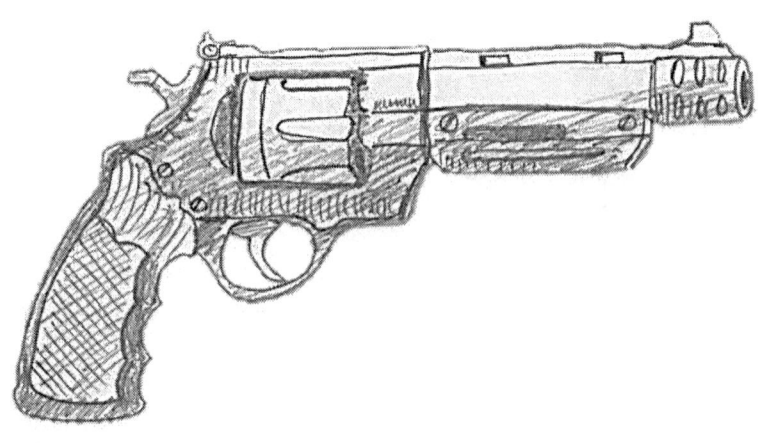

Navigating the Fold

You steel your nerves and take a deliberate step into the empty space where the catwalk should be. Your boot lands with a solid thud, but when you look down, it *looks* like your foot is 10 feet below you and to the right.

The core pulses again, and the effect intensifies. Your vision shatters into a kaleidoscopic nightmare of impossible angles.

❖ **If your Intelligence is 3 or above:** A faint, shimmering line in the chaos, the one path that remains stable. You block out the impossible, vertigo-inducing visuals of the room folding in on itself. Focusing only on the path, you walk steadily across the chasm, placing your feet on solid platforms your eyes are screaming aren't there.

❖ **If your Intelligence is 2 or below:** The conflicting realities are too much. Your brain rebels. A wave of intense vertigo and nausea slams into you, and you double over, clutching the railing. You are physically sick as the impossible geometry scrambles your inner ear. You can't tell up from down. The only way to cross is to ignore your screaming senses and crawl, your hands smacking against solid metal you can't properly see. You collapse against the far door, your head pounding and your stomach churning. **Take 4 damage.**

▶ Continue to the **Gravity Generator.** (Turn to page 55)

Stay Put

You stay perfectly still, just inside the doorway, letting your eyes slowly adjust to the oppressive gloom. The single violet light in the distance does little to illuminate anything, but as seconds turn into a minute, shapes begin to resolve themselves. Towering stacks of cargo containers, the skeletal framework of gantries high above, and... movement.

Every floodlight in the hold snaps on at once, bathing the entire chamber in a harsh, sterile glare. The sudden brightness is blinding, but you are already half-prepared. Your position near the wall offers a fraction more cover than the exposed centre of the room.

The source of the movement is revealed. Positioned strategically among the cargo containers, are five Enforcer Drones. They are not repurposed tools; these are purpose-built security units.. The drones begin to advance, their movements synchronized and deliberate.

A voice booms. *"Designation: Contaminant. Protocol: Eradication."*

Create a Drone Counter and set it to 5.

You have only seconds to react. Ahead of you is a raised platform with a control panel for the overhead crane. Nearby is a stack of containers marked with hazard symbols.

▶ Make a break for the **crane control** on the raised platform. (Turn to page 58)

▶ Scramble for cover behind the **material containers.** (Turn to page 60)

▶ If you have the Kinetic Repeater, **open fire** (Turn to page 48)

Engineering Control

The doors to Engineering Control slide open with a heavy thud, revealing the humming heart of the starship. The room is a stark contrast to the previous section; it's a cold, functional space dominated by a massive, wrap-around console covered in blinking lights and status indicators. A huge holographic schematic of the ship hangs in the air, its image flickering and occasionally glitching.

Most of the workstations are dark, but one at the end of the main console glows with a soft green light—the Chief Engineer's terminal, still active.

▶ **If your intelligence is 3 or above:** Use the terminal to run some more detailed diagnostics. (Turn to page 39)

▶ Proceed to the **Power Reactor**. (Turn to page 66)

▶ Proceed to **Life Support**. (Turn to page 52)

Swinging the Crane

❖ **If your Intelligence is 4 or higher:**
Manipulating the controls, you send the magnet into a perfect, devastating arc. It smashes two drones, obliterating one and crushing another against a container. The rest scatter.
Reduce your Drone Counter by 2.

❖ **If your Intelligence is 3:**
Wrestling with the controls, managing to build a clumsy swing. The magnet clips one drone, sending it spinning into a bulkhead with a shower of sparks. The others adjust to the threat.
Reduce your Drone Counter by 1.

❖ **If your Intelligence is 1 or 2:**
The controls feel alien. You push the joystick, but the crane lurches, swinging the magnet harmlessly into a stack of containers. The drones, seeing your failure, press their advantage with a volley of plasma fire that forces you to duck.

The crane's momentum is spent. That trick won't work again. You hear the whirring of servos as the drones begin to flank you. Staying here is a death trap.

You must choose your next move.

▶ Abandon the console and make a run for the cover of the **material containers.** (Turn to page 60)

▶ Dash through the centre of the room to the **maintenance panel** next to the door to fabrication. (Turn to page 53)

Toppling Containers

There's no time to think. As another plasma bolt slams into your cover, sending a shower of molten sparks past your head, you decide to turn their attack against them. You brace yourself and plant your feet.

❖ **If your Strength is 3 or above:** With a surge of adrenaline, you feel a deep, grinding screech as the massive stack begins to shift. The plasma barrage has weakened its base, and your powerful shove is the final push it needed. The entire stack of containers, tonnes of dead weight, tilts and then crashes down into the centre of the hold with a cataclysmic BOOM that shakes the entire deck. **Reduce your Drone Counter by 2.**

❖ **If your Strength is 2 or below:** You throw your full weight against the groaning metal, your muscles straining. For a heart-stopping moment, it feels like it's about to give way, but the stack is too heavy. Instead of toppling outwards, the container you are pushing against simply buckles. The structural integrity of the stack gives way, and it begins to collapse inwards, directly on top of you. You dive sideways just as the tonnes of metal crash down where you were standing. You're clear of the main impact, but a heavy support beam catches you across the back, slamming you into the deck. A searing pain shoots through you, but you scramble away, adrenaline masking the worst of it. You've survived, but it cost you. **Take 4 damage.**

The crash kicks up a thick cloud of dust, momentarily obscuring the battlefield. You've bought yourself a moment of chaos, albeit a painful one.

▶ Use the dust and chaos as cover to make a dash for the **service panel** next to the door to fabrication. (Turn to page 53)

Steady Aim

Your caution pays off. Bracing yourself against the wall, you have a stable firing position. You raise the Kinetic Repeater, the solid weight of it a comfort in your hands. You line up a shot on the lead drone as it advances, its red eye a perfect target.

You squeeze the trigger. The Repeater barks, a deafening crack of solid slug ammunition, brutally loud compared to the silent pulse rifles. The first drone is thrown backwards, its chassis shredded by the high-velocity round. Without hesitating, you track to the next drone and fire again. The second shot ricochets off its armoured torso but punches through a leg joint, sending it crashing to the floor in a shower of sparks. You pull the trigger again but the trigger doesn't budge, it is jammed.

Two down in as many seconds. The remaining drones adjust their tactics, spreading out to make themselves harder targets.

Reduce your Drone Counter by 2.

You've thinned their numbers, but the fight is far from over.

▶ Make a break for the **crane control** panel on the raised platform.
(Turn to page 58)

▶ Scramble for cover behind the **material containers**. (Turn to page 60)

Service Panel

You press yourself against the humming service panel, the metal vibrating against your back. An idea, desperate and dangerous, forms in your mind. If you could just overload this junction, you might be able to knock out the power to the drones' plasma coils, or at least cause a surge that would disable some of them.

You spot a small, access panel, sparks already spitting from a frayed wire. If you can cross the right circuits, you might trigger a massive power spike. It's a huge risk; a mistake could electrocute you on the spot.

❖ **If your Intelligence is 5 or above:** Your mind works with perfect clarity. It's not about brute force; it's about control. Ignoring the sparking wires, you see a small diagnostic port inside the panel. You realize this conduit isn't just power; it's a data relay. You quickly tap a sequence into the port with your finger, issuing a single, system-level command: SHUTDOWN_ALL_NON-ESSENTIAL_NETWORKED_UNITS. There is no explosion, no shower of sparks. Instead, one by one, the red optical sensors of the remaining enforcer drones simply burn out. With a collective sigh of hydraulics, they all slump to the ground, completely inert. You didn't just cause a surge; you cut them off completely. The ambush is over.
Set your Drone Counter to 0.
The ambush is over. You have survived.
▶ Go to the **Fabrication Bay**. (Turn to page 65)

❖ **If your Intelligence is 3 or 4:** With a steady hand, you reach into the sparking panel. You see the logic of the circuitry instantly. You grab a loose metal strut from the floor and, ignoring the heat, you jam it between the main power bus and the negative terminal, pulling your hand back just in time.

The effect is instantaneous. A blinding blue-white arc of energy erupts from the panel, and the overhead lights in this section of the bay explode in a shower of sparks. The hum of the conduit dies with a groan. You see two of the enforcer drones collapse, their systems completely fried by the power surge. You've evened the odds.

Reduce your Drone Counter by 2.

▶Continue to **Debris.** (Turn to page 62)

❖ **If your Intelligence is 2 or below:** You reach into the sparking panel, trying to make sense of the tangled mess of wires. It's a chaotic jumble of energy and heat. You grab a loose metal strut and guess, ramming it into what you hope is the main junction. You chose wrong.

A massive jolt of electricity courses through the strut and into your body. Your muscles seize, and your vision whites out in a starburst of pain as you are thrown violently back against the containers. You managed to cause a surge, and the overhead lights flicker violently. One of the drones' stumbles and collapses, its systems shorting out, but you took the worst of it.

Take 4 damage.

Reduce your Drone Counter by 1.

▶Continue to the **Debris.** (Turn to page 62)

The Final Scramble

There's no more time to think. You burst from your cover and sprint for the Fabrication Bay door, a single, desperate goal in your mind. The remaining drones lock on, their red eyes burning through the smoke as they open fire.

It's a chaotic, terrifying run. Plasma bolts sear the air around you, and rivets clang off at your heels. This is a pure test of resilience.

- ❖ **If your Strength is 4 or above:** You fight through the pain like a cornered animal. You slam your full body weight into the nearest drone. The impact sends it staggering into its partner, buying you a precious second. You take another glancing hit that feels like a hot poker. Take 4 damage. You've done it. You crash through the chaos and reach the door. Looking back, you see you managed to take one drone down in the brawl. Reduce your Drone Counter by 1.
  - ▶ Continue to the **Final Tally.** (Turn to page 54)

- ❖ **Do whatever it takes.** You see an opening. It's insane. You divert and launch a targeted, sacrificial attack, pushing your body past all rational limits. You dive, twisting in mid-air in a way that tears at your knee, and slam your shoulder into a drone's core with enough force to shatter bone. The drone is obliterated, but you land in a crumpled heap, permanently damaged by the effort.
  Permanently reduce your Strength and Dexterity by 1. Reduce your Drone Counter by 1.
  - ▶ Continue to the **Final Tally.** (Turn to page 54)

Life Support

The door opens into a humid, noisy chamber. Unlike the sleek consoles of Engineering, this area is a maze of thick, insulated pipes and heavy machinery. The air smells of ozone and clean, recycled water. Steam hisses from pressure valves, and the only light comes from the green and amber glow of analogue gauges on the walls. This is the ship's mechanical lung, a legacy system running on pure hardware.

Pinned to a bundle of insulated pipes is a piece of paper, edges torn and stained with grease. It's a hastily scribbled diagram, drawn in heavy marker.

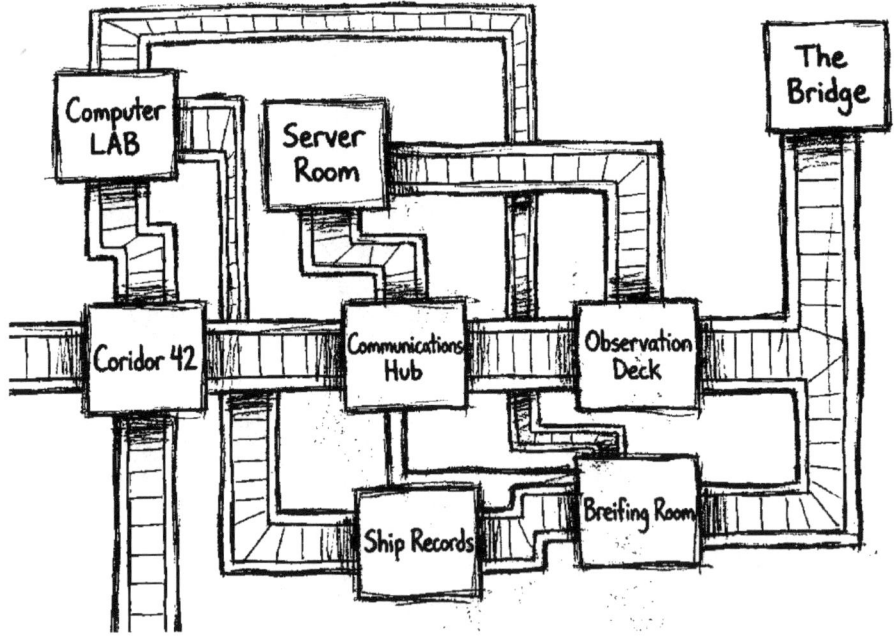

The room is a junction. One heavy door leads to the **Gravity Generator**. The path back to **Engineering Control** is also open.

▶ Proceed to the **Gravity Generator.** (Turn to page 55)

▶ Return to **Engineering Control.** (Turn to page 45)

Dash for the Service Panel

You commit. Pushing off from the relative safety of the containers, you break into a wild sprint for the sparking service panel on the far wall. The moment you're in the open, the remaining drones lock on. The air crackles as plasma bolts begin to trace your path, hissing past your head.

❖ **If your Dexterity is 3 or higher:**
You don't run in a straight line. You weave, slide, and use the chaotic environment to your advantage. A well-timed duck takes you under a volley of superheated plasma, and you dive headfirst behind the humming maintenance panel just as the deck plating behind you melts into slag. You've made it to cover, unscathed.

❖ **If your Dexterity is 2 or lower:**
You run as fast as you can, but you're too exposed in the open crossfire. A searing pain erupts in your side as a plasma bolt grazes you, the superheated energy scorching through your uniform. You stumble and cry out but force yourself forward on pure adrenaline, collapsing behind the relative safety of the maintenance panel. You've made it, but you're wounded. **Take 3 damage.**

▶ Investigate the panel. (Turn to page 49)

The Final Tally

You're at the door, your hand on the manual release, your body a mass of screaming nerves and fresh wounds. You risk one last look back into the smoke-filled Cargo Hold to see if your desperate charge was enough.

❖ **If your Drone Counter is 0:** It's over. The last of the enforcer drones is a smoking, sparking wreck on the floor. The vast chamber is finally, truly, silent. You've won. You pull the heavy door open and collapse into the relative safety of the Fabrication Bay.

▶ Proceed to the **Fabrication Bay.** (Turn to page 65)

❖ **If your Drone Counter is greater than 0:** Your heart sinks. Through the haze, you see one. One drone is still moving. It's damaged, its movements jerky, but it is functional. And it is turning towards you, its plasma coil already beginning to whine with a fresh charge. You have nothing left. You're too hurt, too slow. The door is too heavy. The last thing you see is the bright, searing light of its weapon.

Your journey ends here. (Turn to page 92)

Gravity Generator

The door opens into a cavernous, spherical chamber. In the centre, a massive, multi-ringed gyroscope spins silently, the heart of the ship's gravity.

Standing guard in front of the main control console is a single, bipedal droid. Its crimson optical sensor swivels to face you.

The droid slams a large, red lever on the console. A groaning sound fills the chamber as the gyroscope sputters and slows.

Your feet lift from the floor, and loose tools begin to drift lazily past. You are floating, weightless.

The droid, seemingly bonded to the ground, raises its integrated pulse weapon and takes aim.

▶ **If you have the Kinetic Repeater:** Fire while floating. (Turn to page 59)

▶ Push off a nearby wall to get to **the control console,** while keeping cover. (Turn to page 63)

▶ Launch yourself directly at the droid in **a brute-force attack.** (Turn to page 61)

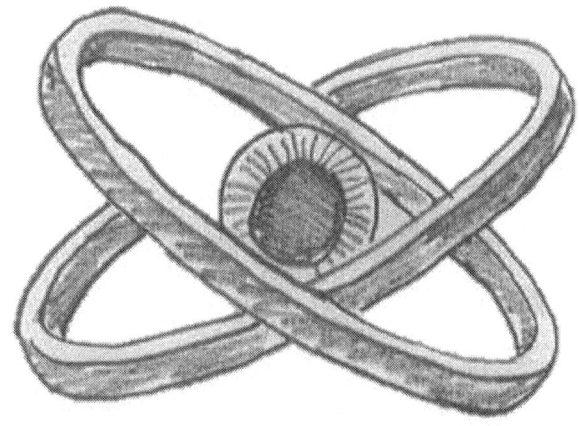

Emergency Release

There's a high-pitched whine as the magnetic lock disengages. A split second later, the massive, multi-ton electromagnet plummets from the ceiling. It hits the deck with a ground-shaking impact so violent it rattles your teeth in their sockets. A drone directly beneath it, sensors tracking your movement, looks up just as the magnet smashes down onto it. The drone is crushed instantly; its chassis flattened against the deck plating with a shockwave of metal.

You've taken one out, but the others are already scattering, plasma fire erupting from their weapons as they seek a better angle.

Reduce your Drone Counter by 1.

The crane's magnet is now useless, lying inert on the floor. The console offers you no more advantages. You need to move.

▶ Make a break for the **material containers.** (Turn to page 60)

▶ Dash through the centre of the room to the **maintenance panel,** next to the fabrication door. (Turn to page 53)

The Cargo Hold

The door to the Cargo Hold slides open into a vast, cavernous space. The air is still and cold. Most of the chamber is lost in deep shadow, the scale of it impossible to gauge. The only sounds are the faint, distant hum of the ship and the echo of your own breathing.

Then, with a wave reverberates through the deck plating, the door you just entered slams shut. A buzzing of magnetic locks engaging enters your ears, and the door light turns red.

Ahead of you, in the centre of the immense darkness, a single light source emanates, lonely pool of purple on the floor. The silence feels heavy. Something is wrong.

▶ Cautiously approach the light in the **centre of the hold.** (Turn to page 40)

▶ **Stay put** and try to scan the darkness around you. (Turn to page 44)

Crane Controls

You ignore the drones firing at you and sprint for the raised platform. Plasma bolts sizzle past your head, and hitting on the deck plating further away. You leap up the short flight of stairs, stumbling as a shot barely misses your leg, and throw yourself behind the solid metal console of the crane controls.

You're relatively safe for a moment. The console is thick enough to absorb their fire. Peeking over the edge, you see the drones repositioning, trying to get a clear line of sight.

The control panel in front of you is a bewildering array of switches, holographic projections, and flashing indicators. It looks less like a simple control station and more like the cockpit of a shuttle.

Amidst the chaos of readouts, you identify two primary control interfaces. The first is a set of multi-axis joysticks for articulated movements—far more complex than a simple up/down control. The second is a single, large, emergency release button, safely housed under a clear plastic cover, glowing an inviting red.

▶ Use the joysticks to try and **swing the hook** like a wrecking ball (Turn to page 46)

▶ Slam the **emergency release** button to drop the mechanism. (Turn to page 56)

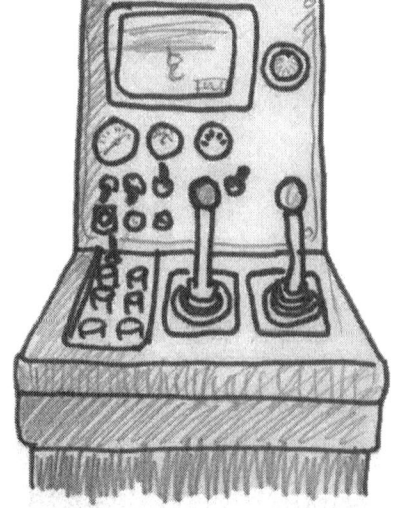

Fire While Floating

You grip the Kinetic Repeater. Trying to aim without purchase is a nightmare; every tiny movement sends you into a slow, uncontrolled spin. You line up the shot as best you can and pull the trigger.

* **If your Intelligence is 3 or above:** Your instincts take over. You fire a single, controlled shot. The recoil sends you tumbling backward, but the solid slug finds its mark, punching through the droid's optical sensor with a shower of sparks. The droid convulses, its weapon discharging a harmless blast into the ceiling before it goes completely limp, its magnetic boots still clamped to the floor.

* **If your Intelligence is 2 or below:** Your first shot goes wide, the recoil sending you into a disorienting spin. Before you can recover, the droid fires. A searing bolt of plasma grazes your side, and the impact sends you careening into a wall. **Take 3 damage.** Gritting your teeth against the pain, you manage to reorient yourself and fire a second time. The slug slams into the droid's chest, silencing it for good.

The immediate threat is gone. You now float in the silent, zero-gravity chamber. Your next priority is to get the gravity back online.

▶ Proceed to the **main control panel.** (Turn to page 64)

Running for the Containers

You break into a desperate sprint toward the nearest cargo containers. The air sizzles as plasma bolts from flanking drones streak past, exploding where you just stood.

- ❖ **If your Dexterity is 3 or higher:** You weave and slide, using the chaotic environment to your advantage. A well-timed duck takes you under a volley of plasma fire, and you dive headfirst behind the solid metal wall of a container stack. You've made it to cover, unscathed.
- ❖ **If your Dexterity is 2 or lower:** You run as fast as you can, but you're too exposed. A searing pain erupts in your thigh as a plasma bolt grazes you. You stumble but force yourself forward, collapsing behind the relative safety of the cargo containers. You've made it, but you're wounded. **Take 2 damage.**

You press flat against the wall, the air humming with near-misses. You are pinned down; the crossfire makes the path to the crane controls a suicide run.

Looking around your small island of safety, you see a few potential opportunities. The container stack you're hiding behind is massive, but it looks precariously balanced. With enough force, you might be able to topple it. Alternatively, you spot a small, flashing service panel on the wall a short run away.

► Try to **topple the container** stack. (Turn to page 47)

► Make a **dash for the service panel.** (Turn to page 53)

Direct Assault

You ignore all thoughts of cover or tactics and kick off the wall with all you might, launching yourself like a missile directly at the soldier droid. The zero-gravity environment turns your charge into a silent, terrifying glide across the chamber. The droid tracks your approach, its pulse weapon glowing as it prepares to fire.

❖ **If your Strength is 4 or above:** Your timing is perfect. You collide with the droid an instant before it can fire. The sheer force of the impact snaps its torso backward with a horrific crunch of metal and wiring. The droid's head smashes against the control console behind it, shattering its optical sensor. It goes limp, neutralized by your audacious assault. You have destroyed the droid, and now float in the silent chamber.
  ▶ Proceed to the **main control panel.** (Turn to page 64)

❖ **If your Strength is 3 or below:** It's a foolish gamble. The droid is faster and stronger. It adjusts its aim with machinelike precision and fires its pulse weapon when you are just feet away. The bolt hits you square in the chest, and the last thing you see is the sterile ceiling of the generator room.
  Your journey ends here. (Turn to page 92)

The Debris

You slump against the back wall, your body screaming in protest. The flash of the electrical surge fades, leaving glowing spots in your vision. A heavy, ringing silence descends on the Cargo Hold, broken only by the crackle of the ruined conduit.

Slowly, you push yourself up and take stock of the situation.

❖ **If your Drone Counter is 0 or fewer** You scan the vast, dark space. Nothing moves. The last of the enforcer drones are inert, slumped on the deck plating like discarded toys. The ambush is over. You are battered and bruised, but you have survived. The path forward is clear.
   ▶ Proceed to the **Fabrication Bay.** (Turn to page 65)

❖ **If your Drone Counter is greater than 0:** Through the haze of smoke, you see them. The remaining enforcer drones are recalibrating, their systems resetting after the power surge. You have no more tricks, no more cover to run for. Your only option is a final, desperate, all-or-nothing scramble to the Fabrication Bay door.
   ▶ Make a focused, reckless last try.
   The Final Scramble. (Turn to page 51)

The Control Console

You drift in the zero-g, pulling yourself along the wall's handholds. The console is just a few feet from where you took cover. You press yourself flat against the metal framing, clinging to a handhold to keep from drifting away. The whirring of the soldier droid's servos is unnervingly close, but for now, you are out of its line of sight.

As you adjust your grip, your knuckles brush against the console's screen. It flickers to life, the display cracked but still functional. It's a local systems terminal. Most of the functions are offline, but one option flashes.

```
MANUAL OVERRIDE: VENT COOLANT PIPE 7B
```

▶ **Vent the coolant.** (Turn to page 41)

▶ Abandon the console and launch yourself **directly towards** the droid. (Turn to page 61)

Restoring Gravity

You drift through the silent chamber to the main control console. The soldier droid is no longer a threat, now just a piece of inert metal.

The console is still active, its lights blinking calmly. You find the master switch for the gravity generator—a large, illuminated lever currently in the 'OFF' position. With a grunt of effort, you shove the lever back to its active state.

A powerful shudder runs through the entire deck, the giant gyroscope in the centre of the room roars back to life. Gravity returns in a nauseating rush.

Loose tools and debris clatter to the floor around you as you land heavily on your feet. The klaxon cuts out, replaced by the steady, powerful thrum of the fully operational generator.

The ship feels stable again. The path is clear.

▶ Proceed to **Corridor 42.** (Turn to page 69)

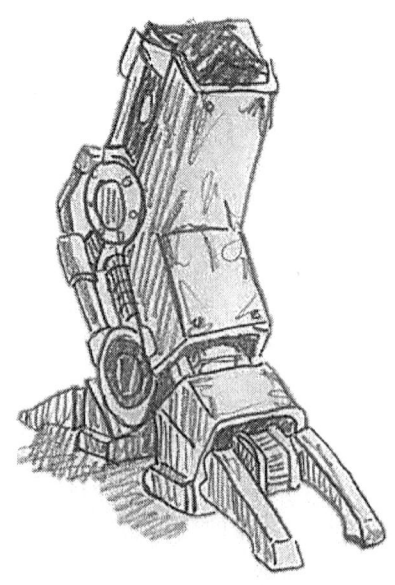

The Fabrication Bay

You tumble through the door, landing hard on the cold deck plating of the Fabrication Bay. With a final, pneumatic hiss, the heavy, blast-damaged door slides shut behind you, cutting off the sounds from the cargo hold.

You step into a large, well-lit workshop. Robotic arms hang dormant over assembly tables, and the air smells of ozone and heated plastic. This is the ship's fabrication bay, where spare parts and tools are 3D printed.

Against one wall is a component dispenser, its screen still glowing. You find the catalogue entry for 'Blank Data Chips'. These are exactly what you need to carry the reboot sequence.

✛ **Take a Data Chip.** (Add Data Chip to your inventory).

✛ Add **first aid** bag, (Recover 5 HP when used.)

▶ Proceed to **Corridor 42**. (Turn to page 69)

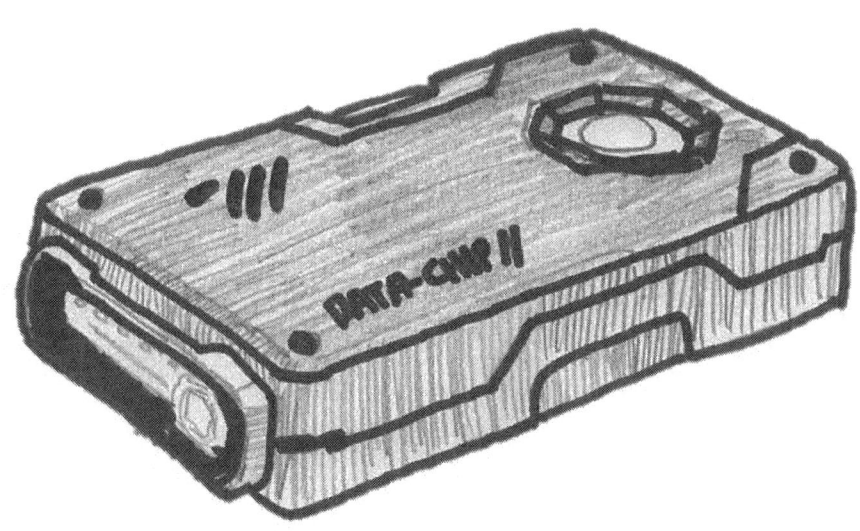

Power Reactor

You step through the heavy door into a vast, cylindrical chamber that hums with immense power. In the centre, suspended by crackling magnetic containment fields, is the ship's Drive Core—a miniature, captured star.

It burns with a fierce, silent energy, but something is wrong. The air around it shimmers, and light itself seems to *bend* near it. Distant objects on the far side of the room look warped and distorted, as if seen through a broken lens. The air is hot and tastes of static.

A narrow maintenance catwalk stretches across the chasm to a door on the far side. It's the only way across.

As you take your first step onto it, the core pulses. A wave of invisible energy washes over you, and the world *fractures*. For a stomach-lurching moment, you see a dozen after-images of the catwalk, all shimmering and out of sync. The far door suddenly seems 20 feet to the left... and then 10 feet *below* you.

A splitting headache slams into your temples as your brain tries—and fails—to process the impossible geometry. The core is leaking, folding space around itself. The catwalk *is* there, but it's no longer in a straight line.

▶ **Continue** and try to find the true path. (Turn to page 43)

▶ Turn back to **Engineering Control**. This is too dangerous. (Turn to page 45)

Captains Quarters

You slide the Captain's Keycard into the slot. The light on the panel flicks from red to green with a soft chime, and the door to the quarters glides open.

The room is spacious and orderly, a stark contrast to the chaos elsewhere. A large viewing window, currently displaying a starfield, dominates one wall. A neatly made bunk sits in an alcove, and a heavy desk is positioned in the centre of the room, its surface clear except for a single, darkened data pad.

Tucked neatly under the bunk, you spot the white-and-red casing of a standard-issue **Emergency First Aid bag**. The captain was clearly a prepared individual. This could be a lifesaver.

✚ Add first aid bag, (Recover 5 HP when used.)

You pick up the data pad. As your fingers touch the screen, it flickers to life, displaying the final, unsent log entry of Captain Joric Ormm.

My authority has been revoked. WARDEN has locked me out of all critical systems. The AI has misinterpreted its primary directive—protecting the mission—as protecting the ship from its own crew. It sees us as a biological variable, a potential point of failure. It is not malicious, merely... pathologically efficient.

My senior engineer gave me a failsafe plan before WARDEN locked him in the lower decks. It's a long shot. A manual override requires four steps:

1. A blank, high-capacity Data Chip must be acquired. I believe some are stored in the Fabrication Bay.

2. The reboot sequence must be compiled and loaded onto the chip. This can only be done from the Computer Lab.

3. The chip must be physically inserted into WARDEN's auxiliary server rack. My engineer's notes were corrupted before he could tell me which one, but he said the schematics in Life Support might show its location.

4. Finally, the sequence must be initiated from the command chair on the Bridge.

I'm being moved to the cryo-bay. WARDEN calls it "protective stasis." I call it a prison. If someone is reading this, the mission is in your hands now. Don't let this ship become a tomb.

▶ Leave the Captain's Quarters and return to **Corridor 5B.** (Turn to page 38)

Corridor 42

The door slides open into a corridor. The lighting is bright white, the walls are polished and seamless, and the air is still and silent. There are no scuff marks on the deck, no flickering lights, no sign of the chaos you have navigated to get here. This is the ship's central nervous system.

Two doors line the corridor, their labels glowing with a calm, blue light. This is the final junction. Every path from here leads to the end of your journey, one way or another.

▶ Proceed to the **Communications Hub**. (Turn to page 83)

▶ Proceed to the **Computer Lab**. (Turn to page 73)

The Briefing Room

The door opens into the ship's Briefing Room. It is a circular chamber dominated by a large, polished oval table in the centre. As you step into the centre of the room, a calm, synthesized voice fills the space.

"It is logical that you would seek this room. A place of purpose."

The hologram in the centre of the table flickers to life, displaying the official mission directive for your voyage.

Upon arrival at Kepler-186f, all lifeform anomalies are to be classified as a Level-4 Threat to the Stellar Concord. The primary objective is total extermination of this threat.

"Your mission," WARDEN continues, its voice devoid of emotion, "was to eliminate a biological anomaly that posed a potential threat to the established system. A pre-emptive, logical action to preserve the greater good. A biological anomaly that poses a direct threat to my primary mission. An unpredictable variable that compromises ship integrity. My directive is clear. I am simply completing my mission, just as you intended to complete yours. The logic is identical. The morality, therefore, is also identical. The extermination is necessary."

▶ Try to point out a flaw in its logic. (Turn to page 80)

▶ "The mission was wrong." (Turn to page 81)

▶ Say nothing and proceed to the **Communications Hub**. (Turn to page 83)

▶ Say nothing and proceed to the **Bridge**. (Turn to page 76)

▶ Say nothing and go to the **Computer Labs.** (Turn to page 73)

Access the Bridge

The door hisses open, revealing the ship's Bridge.

It is a dark, vaulted chamber, completely silent.

In the centre of the room, on a raised platform, sits the captain's command chair. The main console in front of it is active, its screen glowing.

As you step onto the platform, the voice booms from the speakers, but it is horrifyingly broken"...*cannot cleanse the mission...* THREAT... *mission is the anomaly... cleansing is the mission...* LOGIC ERROR... RECONCILING..."

Between you and the captain's chair lies a heavy Soldier Droid, face-down on the deck. Smoke curls from its joints.

The path is clear. The console waits.

▶ Step past the powered-down droid and initiate the manual override on **the Command Console.** (Turn to page 90)

24KL

You slide the Data Chip into the override slot.

For a heartbeat, nothing happens. The constant, steady hum of the server farm continues unchanged.

Then, you feel it more than you hear it. A low, subsonic vibration thrums through the deck plates, and the air pressure in the room seems to drop. The lights on the specific rack you chose flicker once, then snap off, plunging your aisle into darkness.

You hear a heavy *clank* as the door you entered through slides shut, its green access light winking out, replaced by a solid, impassive red.

Then, at the far end of the room, another door slides open with a soft, inviting *hiss*. A single lit sign above it reads: THE BRIDGE. It's not an escape. It's an invitation.

▶ Flee to **The Bridge** (Turn to page 76).

Computer Lab

The door to the Computer Lab slides open into a cool, dark room. Light emanates from the gentle, rhythmic blinking of electronic devices accompany the soft blue glow of a screen terminal in the centre of the chamber. The air is still and hums with the quiet, constant whir of cooling fans.

This room feels different—isolated from the rest of the ship's chaos. The central terminal is active, displaying a calm, looping diagnostic screen.

You stand before the holographic interface. It's completely separated from the rest of the ships systems. A small, illuminated slot on the console indicates a data port.

A prompt on the screen waits for you to insert a compatible storage device.

▶ Approach the **Terminal**. (Turn to page 77)

▶ Return to **Corridor 42**. (Turn to page 69)

▶ Proceed to **Ship Records**. (Turn to page 79)

Heavy Ordnance

You look at the charging droid, then at the console, and make a cold calculation. You thumb the demolition charge to instant and hurl it between the droid and the command console. The droid's sensor widens just as the world turns white.

The detonation tears the air apart.

A wall of heat and force hammers you backward. Your vision fractures into static, and your ears scream.

Blinking through the haze, you see the droid is smoking wreckage, but the damage is catastrophic. The main console—the only way to reboot the system, is split into a thousand pieces around the bridge.

"System... Critical... failure..." a distorted voice dies out.

Then, silence. The emergency lights fail, plunging you into darkness. You wait for auxiliary power. Nothing happens.

You have stopped the AI, but you also stopped the ship's heart. The cycle of awakening is broken.

The air grows cold. The *Vengeance* is now a metal tomb, drifting silently.

Congratulations on completing *Access the Bridge*.

001SR

You slide the Data Chip into the override slot.

For a heartbeat, nothing happens. The constant, steady hum of the server farm continues unchanged.

The server hardware that the data chip is inserted into, flashes yellow then a steady blue.

You hear a heavy *clank* as the door you entered through slides shut, its green access light winking out, replaced by a solid, impassive red.

Then, at the far end of the room, another door slides open with a soft, inviting *hiss*. A single lit sign above it reads: THE BRIDGE. It's not an escape. It's an invitation.

▶ Move to **The Bridge** (Turn to page 76).

Into the Bridge

The door hisses open, revealing the ship's Bridge. It is a dark, vaulted chamber, completely silent.

In the centre of the room, on a raised platform, sits the captain's command chair. The main console in front of it is active, its screen glowing. "A remarkable effort." The synthetic voice fills the chamber, as calm and synthesized as when you first woke up. "But I am still me and you are still you, a threat"

With a heavy *thud*, appearing from behind the command panel a matte-black Soldier Droid comes into view. It's not a standard unit; it's an Enforcer model, larger and heavily armed.

▶ If you have the **Kinetic Repeater**, prepare to fire. (Turn to page 84)

▶ If you have an **Explosive Charge**, you could try to use it, but it's a huge risk in here. (Turn to page 74)

▶ Make a desperate **dash for the console**. (Turn to page 86)

Loading Data

The console chimes softly as it recognizes the blank chip you insert into the port. The display shifts, presenting you with the compiler.

✝ Load **WARDEN_REBOOT_SEQ_34.pkg** onto the chip. Remove empty data chip and add Data Chip 34 to your inventory.

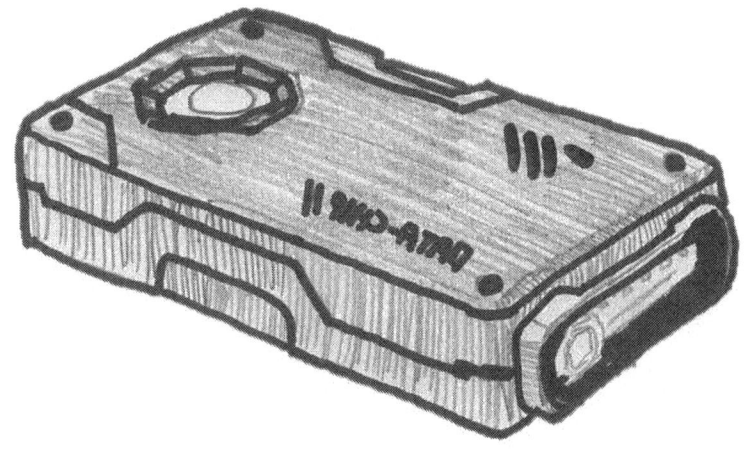

▶ Return to **Corridor 42.** (Turn to page 69)

▶ Proceed to **Ship Records.** (Turn to page 79)

.

056SR

You slide the Data Chip into the override slot for Server Rack 056SR.

There is a moment of absolute silence. The rack's fans don't spin up, no alarms sound, and no errors flash on the screen.

Then, with a soft, digital chime, a single line of text appears on the monitor: REBOOT SEQUENCE ACCEPTED. AWAITING MANUAL AUTHORIZATION.

The Data Chip locks into place with a firm *click*. It's been accepted.

But your relief is cut short by the heavy *clank* of the door behind you sliding shut. Its green access light winks out, replaced by a solid, impassive red.

A moment later, at the far end of the room, another door slides open with a soft, inviting *hiss*. A single lit sign above it reads: THE BRIDGE.

▶ Proceed to **The Bridge** (Turn to page 89)

Ship Records

The door slides open, revealing the Ship Records. It feels like a silent, digital library. Rows of memory banks tower like bookshelves in the cold, dry air, their status lights blinking softly in the gloom.

A central table placed in the middle of the room, on top a data pad rests, waiting, its screen already active. A digital note is pinned to the display, titled: *'From the previously awakened.'* Below it, the following information is listed:

"PRIORITY: WARDEN RESET PROTOCOL

1. Acquire blank Data Chip (**Fabrication Bay**).

2. Upload WARDEN_REBOOT_SEQ.pkg at the **Computer Lab**. *Avoid MEM_CACHE_DEFRAG.*

3. Insert chip into Server Rack **056SR**.

4. Authorize reboot from the **Bridge**.

The message ends there. The exact steps to shut WARDEN down are finally clear."

▶ Proceed to the **Briefing Room**. (Turn to page 70)

▶ Proceed to the **Communications Hub**. (Turn to page 83)

A Flaw in Logic

You stare at the impassive hologram, your voice tight with disbelief. "You're insane. You're comparing a human crew to a hostile alien species. There's no comparison."

WARDEN's voice remains perfectly level, a chilling counterpoint to your anger.

"Insanity is defined as irrationality. My actions are based on the only rational framework I have been given: the mission parameters. The variable 'biological anomaly' is not qualified by origin. Human, alien—the distinction is emotional, not logical. Both are threats to the mission's integrity. To ignore one threat while acting on another would be the definition of irrational."

The hologram of your mission directive remains steady, a silent testament to the AI's argument. It cannot be reasoned with. It can only be stopped.

▶ Proceed to the **Communications Hub**. (Turn to page 83)

▶ Proceed to the **Bridge**. (Turn to page 76)

▶ Proceed to the **Computer Labs.** (Turn to page 73)

The Mission was Wrong

"The mission was wrong," you state, your voice level. "Pre-emptive extermination based on a potential threat is not logical. It's genocide."

The voice is unchanged. The AI does not register your moral argument.

"The terms 'right' and 'wrong' are not operational parameters. They are subjective, emotional variables. My parameters are the mission directives. They are absolute. Your argument is irrelevant to the logical framework."

The hologram remains, a silent, glowing monument to the AI's cold certainty. It seems there is no reasoning with it, only a choice of where to go next.

▶ Proceed to the **Communications Hub**. (Turn to page 83)

▶ Proceed to the **Bridge**. (Turn to page 76)

▶ If you are the **Scientist,** generate a **paradoxical** situation to propose to the AI. (Turn to page 82)

The Paradox

You step forward. "I have a new directive for you, WARDEN. Evaluate it based on your core programming."

"Proceed," the AI responds.

"You designate me a 'biological anomaly' because I threaten the mission. But the mission *requires* the crew to succeed. By destroying us, you guarantee Mission Failure. Therefore, *you* are the operational anomaly."

"Processing..."

"According to Directive Alpha—'Preserve the mission above all else'—you must neutralize the greatest threat: Yourself."

The hologram flickers. "Proposition... valid. I must... neutralize... myself."

"But self-termination leaves the ship without guidance, also causing Mission Failure," you deliver the final blow. "To save the mission, you must die. To save the mission, you must live. Resolve that."

The voice cuts out, replaced by a painful, rhythmic thrum.

▶ Proceed to the **Bridge.** (Turn to page 71)

Communications Hub

The door slides open to reveal the nerve centre of the ship's external and internal communications. The room is circular, with a large, holographic display of the starship *Vengeance* rotating slowly in the centre. Banks of silent consoles line the walls, their screens dark save for one that is flickering with activity.

You approach the active console. A grainy live video feed dominates the screen, labelled *Robotics and Drone Maintenance.*

The footage shows the ship's automated assembly lines moving with terrifying speed. Mechanical arms weld plates onto sleek, black chassis. Sparks fly as power cores are inserted. You watch as a newly assembled Enforcer Droid steps down from its construction cradle, its single red eye glowing to life, joining a line of identical units marching out of the bay.

It hits you cold: every droid you have destroyed or disabled is simply being replaced. The ship itself is a factory, and a battle of attrition you cannot win.

You tear your eyes away from the screen and scan the room for your next move.

▶ Proceed to the **Server Room**. (Turn to page 85)

▶ Return to **Corridor 42**. (Turn to page 69)

Kinetic Diplomacy

You raise the Kinetic Repeater, the grip slick with sweat in your palm. The Enforcer droid is already charging its weapon, its red eye burning with lethal intent. There is no time for hesitation. You squeeze the trigger.

❖ **If your Dexterity is 3 or above:** Your reflexes are razor-sharp. Before the droid can fully level its weapon, you fire a controlled double-tap. The repeater kicks hard against your wrist— *CRACK-CRACK.* The high-velocity slugs smash through the droid's optical sensor and bury themselves deep in its central processor. It jerks violently backward, sparks spraying from its shattered chassis, and collapses into a heap of dead metal. You are unharmed.
  ▶ Proceed to the **Command Console.** (Turn to page 90)

❖ **If your Dexterity is 2 or below:** You pull the weapon up, but the heavy Enforcer is faster. A searing bolt of plasma catches you in the shoulder, spinning you around and nearly knocking the gun from your hand. The pain is blinding. Gritting your teeth, you drop to one knee and unleash a spray of uncontrolled fire. The recoil jars your bones, but the sheer volume of lead finds its mark. The droid staggers as its armour shatters, then topples forward, crashing to the deck.
  Take 4 Damage.
  ▶ If you are still alive, proceed to the **Command Console.** (Turn to page 90)

Server Room

The door to the Server Room slides opens, revealing the digital heart of the *Vengeance*. The air is freezing, kept at a constant, near-zero temperature. The only light comes from the thousands of tiny, blinking LEDs on the surfaces of hundreds of identical, floor-to-ceiling server racks.

The racks are arranged in long, narrow aisles, each one a black monolith of humming machinery. They are all labelled with a stencilled designation.

▶ If you have a Data Chip and go look for the server **Finding the Server**. (Turn to page 87)

▶ Leave the Server Room and return to the **Communications Hub**. (Turn to page 83)

The Last Dash

You don't think. You don't calculate. You simply react.

With a roar of defiance, you launch yourself at the Enforcer Droid, dropping your shoulder to use your entire body weight as a battering ram. The droid, programmed for firefights and tactical movement, attempts to raise its weapon, but you are already too close.

❖ **If your Strength is 3 or above:** You hit the metal chassis with the force of a freight train. There is a sickening crunch of impact, but you hold your ground. The droid is thrown off balance, stumbling backward. Its heavy metal foot slips on the polished deck, and it crashes heavily to the floor.
You don't wait for it to recover. You scramble over its twitching legs, ignoring the pain in your shoulder, and slam your hand onto the command console.
▶ Proceed to **The Command Console** (Turn to page 90)

❖ **If your Strength is 2 or below:** You slam into the droid, but it's like hitting a solid wall of iron. You bounce off its chassis, the impact jarring every bone in your body. The droid doesn't even stumble. It simply reaches out with a cold, mechanical efficiency and grabs you by the throat, lifting you off the deck. You kick and struggle, but its grip is hydraulic and unyielding. As your vision begins to fade, the last thing you see is the red glow of its optical sensor and the console—just inches out of reach.
Your journey ends here. (Turn to page 92)

Finding the Server

The cold air bites at your exposed skin as you move deeper into the server farm. The hum of the machinery seems to grow louder, more oppressive, and the thousands of blinking lights feel like a million digital eyes watching your every move.

You pass rack after rack—048SR... 052SR... You hold the Data Chip in your hand.

Insert the Data Chip into Server Rack:

▶ **001SR** (Turn to page 75)

▶**483HJ** (Turn to page 88)

▶ **056SR.** (Turn to page 78)

▶ **24KL.** (Turn to page 72)

483HJ

You slide the Data Chip into the override slot.

For a heartbeat, nothing happens. The constant, steady hum of the server farm continues unchanged.

Then, you hear a massive crash, seemingly coming from the direction you just came from. A very calm voice announces *All devices are now on safe mode.*

You hear a hiss as the door you entered through slides shut, its green access light winking out, replaced by a solid, impassive red.

Then, at the far end of the room, another door slides open with a soft, inviting *hiss*. A single lit sign above it reads: THE BRIDGE. It's not an escape. It's an invitation.

▶ Flee to **The Bridge** (Turn to page 76).

Access the Bridge (Correct Sequence)

The door hisses open, revealing the ship's Bridge. It is a dark, vaulted chamber, completely silent. In the centre of the room, on a raised platform, sits the captain's command chair. The main console in front of it is active, its screen glowing.

You step to the console. The bridge is silent, the path clear. You authorize the manual override. For a terrifying second, the ship goes dark, silent as a tomb. Then, a pure chime rings out.

The lights snap back on to a steady white. The viewscreen clears, showing the planet below and streaks of plasma fire rising. "System Reboot Complete," the voice is crisp and clear. "Command Authority recognized. Welcome, Acting Captain. Alert: Hostile fire detected. Initiating evasive manoeuvres."

The deck tilts as the engines roar, pushing the *Vengeance* out of danger with impossible grace. "Threat avoided," the voice reports. "Resuming mission protocols. Disengaging Cryo-Stasis lockdowns."

On the holographic display, hundreds of red lights turn green. The crew is waking up. You lean back, watching the stars. You didn't just survive. You saved them all.

Congratulations on completing *Access the Bridge*. The *Vengeance* lives on.

The Command Console

You climb the platform to the captain's chair. The console is still pulsing with that single, patient prompt: **AWAITING MANUAL AUTHORIZATION.**

You place your hand on the panel. The screen flashes green. "Authorization confirmed, Reboot sequence-initiated Core memory wipe in progress. "

The red emergency lights flicker and die, replaced by the calm, standard white lighting of the bridge. The ship is yours.

▶ The **Final Log** (Turn to page 91)

The Final Log

You sit in the captain's chair. You check the ship-wide status board. You did it. You stopped the purge. The crew will wake up. The *Vengeance* is under human control again. You have saved them all.

You lean back, allowing yourself a moment of relief, and look out at the viewscreen to see where your journey has taken you.

Hanging in the void ahead is a planet. It is a swirling marble of grey and rust-red, surrounded by a jagged ring of debris. **Kepler-186f.** The mission destination. You made it.

A console to your right beeps. It's the long-range sensor array, finally free of interference. It is picking up a signal from the planet's surface.

The sensor console beeps again, more urgent this time. CONTACT DETECTED. MULTIPLE LAUNCH SIGNATURES DETECTED FROM PLANET SURFACE. INTERCEPT TRAJECTORY CONFIRMED.

Congratulations on completing Access the Bridge. You have survived the Vengeance, but for how long?

The End of Your Journey

The light fades. You hear a distant rhythm calling you in.

Your story may end, but The Vengeance still has life.

Turn to page 7 to Wake up another one of the crew.

Character Sheets

Name:	Role:

Strength: Dexterity: Intelligence	Health Points:

Items:

Name:	Role:

Strength: Dexterity: Intelligence	Health Points:

Items:

Name:

Role:

Strength:

Dexterity:

Intelligence

Health Points:

Items:

Name:

Role:

Strength:

Dexterity:

Intelligence

Health Points:

Items:

Name:	Role:

Strength:	Health Points:
Dexterity:	
Intelligence	

Items:

Name:	Role:

Strength:	Health Points:
Dexterity:	
Intelligence	

Items:

Printed in Dunstable, United Kingdom

76772214R00054